TALES FROM SPACESHIP EARTH

Tales From Spaceship Earth

Blue Marble Space Institute of Science
Short Story Collection
Volume 1

Habitable Press

Cover design by San Francisco-based
artist Rachel Diaz-Bastin, using colored pencils.
http://racheldiazbastin.com

Blue Marble Space Institute of Science
1001 4th Ave, Suite 3201, Seattle WA 98154, USA
http://www.bmsis.org

This book contains works of fiction. Names, characters, businesses, places, events, and incidents are either the products of the author's imagination or used in a fictitious manner. Any resemblance to actual persons, living or dead, or actual events is purely coincidental. The authors do not express the opinions of BMSIS.

Printed in the United States of America
First Printing: March 2016

ISBN-10: 0692605037
ISBN-13: 978-0692605035

"Imagination will often carry us to worlds that never were. But without it we go nowhere."

—*Carl Sagan*

CONTENTS

PREFACE

Space exploration can capture our imagination as we aspire toward a future where technology plays an ever-increasing role in transforming our lives. The spirit of exploration that drove human pioneers to cross mountains, deserts, and oceans in search of new ways of life continues to turn our mind toward the resources of space as possible abodes for living. We have just begun to dip our toes into the vast cosmic sea in which our Earth remains afloat, and we still have much to learn about where the current will take us.

Fiction can anticipate progress in science, projecting bold yet plausible strides of a future that often resonates with our experiences today. The short stories in this volume are all written by research scientists at the Blue Marble Space Institute of Science, reflecting an intersection of each author's knowledge of science and vision of the future. These unique perspectives range from the near-term evolution of the space station program, to the beginnings of martian colonies, to the ultimate end of life on Earth—all of which grapple with critical issues of our transformation into a spacefaring society. Science provides us with a lens for viewing possibilities of the future, but storytelling allows us to embed these visions into the landscape of human history. Space is still full of surprises, and as we venture farther outward we are certain to discover more about ourselves.

Jacob Haqq-Misra
Clayton, Delaware
December 2015

EOL

Sanjoy M. Som

April 24, 2025

It was a gorgeous spring afternoon in New York City. Under a light breeze and wispy clouds, eight autonomous yellow taxipods were idling, waiting for the astronaut delegation at their hotel near JFK International Airport. American astronaut Sonali Williams, and her friend Lucia Primova from the Russian Federation, stepped into the nearest pod and took a seat facing one another. These new, two-person vehicles were meant to transform public transit in New York City, amidst much outcry from taxi drivers. A map appeared on the side panel with a pleasing voice chiming in: "Please select your destination."

Williams tapped the glowing green circle labeled 'United Nations'—the end of the line. Off they went, following closely behind a snaking line of taxipods, speeding by the bumper to bumper traffic that led into the airport. Primova jumped with a start when the pod suddenly lifted into the air. Williams laughed. "And you call yourself a MiG pilot? Look above you, the taxipod just connected with the maglev rail," she informed. "We're on the 'pod green line, which avoids all the traffic and intersection delays, moving at a continuous 45 mph through New York. This is the city's first taxipod line; it connects the airport to the UN with three stops in between. It's revolutionizing public transit."

Primova grumbled, "I don't trust robot pilots. Robots are meant to help, not control."

They were still discussing the role of robotics in transportation when the taxipod reconnected with the asphalt and detached from the magnetic levitation rail. The electric motor powering the wheels whizzed to life taking over propulsion from the rail. It turned one last corner and stopped abruptly in front of the UN building where security guards stood stoic. The astronauts slid out and the taxipod zipped away.

Eol was to be unveiled today with much fanfare. The world's media had converged on New York City to witness the dedication of humankind's first interplanetary habitat. Williams disapproved of these high-profile events, where she felt more like a prop for politicians due to her status as a veteran astronaut, than a true United Nations delegate invited for her intellectual contribution. Primova, on the other hand, was enjoying herself. She was jubilantly waving at the continuous barrage of flash photography. Having recently become the first female Russian commander of the International Space Station a few months back, she was still quite the celebrity—and she knew it.

Meanwhile, one-hundred and fifty miles north, a small explosion startled the sleepy town of Gilboa.

Gilboa lies near the Catskill/Delaware watershed that supplies New York City's water. Together with the Delaware River basin, these watersheds supply 18.3 million people with potable water—making this the largest unfiltered water supply in the world. Yet, the region is also rich in another commodity: natural gas. Drilling crews, despite their precautions, did not realize they were extracting gas from rocks that concealed a geological fault. With the stresses of the fracking process, compounded by the weakened fault, the shale rock fractured intensely, releasing more gas than the exploratory rig could handle. The explosion severely injured two rig workers, but the breach was quickly sealed. Local papers reported a 'drilling irregularity' had occurred near Gilboa. Within days, leisure boaters on the Schoharie Reservoir reported intermittent bubbling on the water's surface. The extent of the pollution was not understood until a peak in migraine headaches reported in New York City was traced back to the contaminated water. In the wake of this seemingly small explosion, America's prosperity would be forever altered.

August 1, 2032

"Trois.. deux.. unité.. top. Allumage Vulcain, allumage EAP, décollage."

"Merde," said Cousteau. He pushed himself away from the main communication console. From their vantage point, one hundred and fifty miles above the Earth's surface, mission specialists Clément Cousteau and Douglas Manchester, and commander Sonali Williams could not hear the roar of the Vulcain main engine and the two 'Etage d'Accéleration à Poudre.' These engines propelled the last Ariane V rocket and its payload, the Autonomous Transfer Vehicle, or ATV, towards their home for the past 32 days, the International Space Station.

"ISS, this is Houston; *Kelvin* is on its way. Docking expected in 6 hours and 12 minutes."

The Europeans named all their ATVs after great historical scientists. *Kelvin* was the second ATV launched in the past month. ATV *Gauss* had docked with ISS shortly after the crew arrived and they had been busy filling it with decommissioned equipment and trash.

"Copy that, Houston," replied Williams.

"Station egress is on schedule at 23:32 UTC tomorrow. Good work today, lads. Now, go get some rest. Tomorrow is a big day."

Manchester reached for the console to switch off the French broadcast. "I suppose it's fitting," he paused, "that the ATVs to bring down ISS are *Gauss* and *Kelvin*".

"Why?" Cousteau inquired in a strained voice revealing his anxiety. He continued without giving his flight companions a chance to respond, "I suppose it's because Gauss streamlined the relationships of orbital mechanics that brought ATV *Gauss* here, and Kelvin quantified the concept of entropy that will roast this outpost?"

"Well, technically, it's not really entropy that..." started Manchester matter-of-factly before Williams twitched, interrupting him. Their eyes locked. Manchester felt an eternity had passed before she averted her gaze. She continued to Cousteau, "Clément, sometimes I wish you had the eloquence that your grandfather had."

"My grandfather died the year after his vessel sank," retorted Cousteau bitterly. "My vessel, this beautiful Space Station, is sinking in three days so allow me to be upset." Cousteau was referring to his ancestor Jacques-Yves Cousteau who sailed the world's oceans in the twentieth century aboard his ship, the *Calypso*, to catalog and promote ocean life and diversity.

The words of Houston were still ringing in Williams' head: "Egress is on schedule." This was her third mission aboard the International Space Station, and her last. She loved it up here. The sense of freedom while unlatched from gravity, the immense spectacle of the space-scape that she would take in after the rigors of daily ops. This is where she felt complete.

A native of Chinsurah, a village thirty miles north of Kolkata, India, Williams spent her youth on the banks of the Hooghly River, a distributary of the sacred Ganges, as the only child of a fisherman widower who desperately wanted a son. The day she escaped down the river on a makeshift barge to evade her abusive father at the age of twelve was the day her life changed for good.

"Your grandfather was one of the greatest explorers the world has ever seen," she said. "I am reminded of his words every time I reach Station; they have been engraved in my memory since childhood."

From birth, man carries the weight of gravity on his shoulders. He is bolted to Earth. But man has only to sink beneath the surface and he is free.

Cousteau smiled with a mix of pride and nostalgia, yet his grimace quickly returned. "You are right—let's enjoy our last day of freedom. What future awaits us space explorers?" he said pensively.

"Dinner," interjected Manchester. "Finest bangers and rehydrated mash this side of the galaxy, I say."

Douglas Manchester, a Liverpool native, was the

jovial kind. Even though he was irked by the sexism in Cousteau's quote, he swallowed these feelings and strived to maintain his smile. He was the person who sought a positive spin in every situation. Williams had specifically requested Manchester for her crew. She valued his natural enthusiasm and optimism, and, coupled with his deep knowledge of spacecraft systems, she considered him the ideal crew-member. A graduate of Cranfield University with a Ph.D. in Systems Engineering, Manchester was part of the 2026 ESA Astronaut class, but had never flown before this mission. In fact, he was the first of that class to fly to the Station. Most of his classmates had left the corps to pursue careers in the commercial sector—a popular destination for novice and veteran astronauts alike. "Not for me," he had always chanted. "Humankind is destined for long duration spaceflight, and I want to be part of it."

The mood was somber at dinner. "This is our last meal on the International Space Station," remarked Williams. "After Doug and I are done with tomorrow's space walks, the Station will no longer be international."

Tomorrow, their thirty-third day aboard humankind's most ambitious engineering feat will come to an end. Returning to the Dragon capsule, they will leave ISS forever. After a few hours, both ATV's will fire their engines, slowing down the mighty space laboratory. Its orbital altitude will decrease to intersect Earth's atmosphere, further slowing the Station down. The high orbital speed coupled with the increasing air density will cause friction to start heating the Station. Devoid of any heat shield, the Station will breakup under the re-entry stress and burn to pieces. Weighing over 500 tons, some large pieces will inevitably survive re-entry, so Station engineers devised a controlled re-entry, expecting the orbital outpost to enter the atmosphere 200 miles south east of Okinawa, Japan. The last pieces will splash into the South Pacific seventeen minutes later.

But this would not be the fate of the entire Station.

The following day, the astronauts were to detach the Russian Orbital Segments (ROS) modules from the ISS. "It feels like a forced separation," said Cousteau. "The *Zarya* and *Unity* modules were linked in 1998. Tomorrow, after forty-four years, they will be forced to separate, with one sibling dying soon after. Ugh." The on-orbit linking of *Zarya*, the first Russian module, and *Unity*, the first American module, heralded the birth of the International Space Station.

The ROS is composed of the *Zarya*, *Zvezda*, *Pirs*, *Poisk*, and *Rassvet* modules, and handles the guidance, navigation, and control of the entire space laboratory. These modules will be the first components of *Eol*. Indeed, ROS will be complemented by a planned larger habitat module, two *Apollo*-style landers, an aquaponics module, and two propulsion modules. At least that was the current plan.

"I hate politicians," Cousteau breathed. "Thirteen months ago, this laboratory was full of scientific experiments. I still can't believe your President canceled the program," his voice was filling with resentment.

"Yes, but there was no longer a backlog of experiments. You know funding has been diverted from ISS to *Eol* by an act of Congress with financial support of the Russians, Japanese, Indians, and Europeans," Williams noted calmly.

"Lads, we should be thankful. ISS was due to deorbit in 2020. Wise were the decision makers to give the Station another twelve years," added Manchester with his trademark optimism. "It's clear these other space agencies want more say in the future of long duration space flight. The Americans didn't plan on taking the lead for *Eol*, and I'm still not convinced they can afford it given the environmental problems plaguing the country. Something must change," he continued.

"Although I don't like admitting this," Cousteau interjected, "ISS was successful because of the American leadership. I am skeptical about a multilateral committee making the decisions. The Americans, Russians, Asians and Europeans… too much baggage. You all know how inefficient the UN is, and let's not even start with what's left of the European Union."

"I agree with Doug. Something has to change," interrupted Williams, not letting herself get derailed by Cousteau's common tangent on the dangers of globalization and pitfalls of international collaboration. "The problem is that *Eol* is too ambitious. It's going to be a program like ITER, the International Thermonuclear Reactor. The reactor is still under construction in France and the agreements were laid down almost half a century ago," she added.

OPSEK, the conceptual predecessor to *Eol*, was an idea spear-headed by Russia almost twenty years ago. The United States didn't seem interested at first, but in the last seven years, as Russia's economy was collapsing under decades of wasteful spending and corruption, the United States accepted leadership after years of congressional debate, renaming the program *Eol*—a gesture of good faith as *Eol* was the Russian translation of Aeolus, the ruler of the winds in the Greek mythology and the name NASA had originally selected for the program following a nationwide contest. It was to be humankind's first trans-planetary and long-duration habitat.

At the program launch ceremony in New York City, *Eol* was heralded as a new beginning for humankind—as groundbreaking as the invention of the Caravelle that allowed fifteenth and sixteenth century European sailors long-duration sea voyages without the need to keep coastlines in sight. Similarly, *Eol* would allow twenty-first century human explorers to embark on long-duration space voyages without the need to keep Earth in sight.

Explorative excursions beyond Earth's orbit had been achieved in the past decade on the *Orion-*

ATV missions. This system was composed of the American *Orion* crew vehicle attached to a modified European ATV serving as the habitat and propulsive units. Such configuration had enabled astronauts to successfully visit near-Earth asteroids, and a proposed journey to Mars was under review. However, such missions were conceived more as reconnaissance than true exploration. Supplies were limited for specific exploration targets, constraining flexibility beyond the planned mission. *Eol* was to be the first *exploration* vehicle capable of multi-year excursions without resupply.

US politicians knew that the ISS was on its last legs. Maintenance costs had been escalating for some time. Also, China's space station was taking shape and its in-space configuration puzzled many experts. US politicians were desperate for the decommissioning of the ISS to ramp up funding for *Eol*. "It's a matter of national security," was the common echo in the corridors of Washington, D.C., which reverberated in the halls of NASA Headquarters. Furthermore, NASA's Space Launch System rocket needed a *raison d'être*. The rocket's full capabilities were rarely utilized by customers and was regularly out-contracted by cheaper, heavy-lift vehicles manufactured by private companies. SLS had been active for fifteen years, yet only three *Orion*-ATV missions had launched. Described as a 'money-sink' in a prominent op-ed column, the program was under consideration for cancellation due to the rising costs associated with the 2025 water catastrophe. Poorly regulated natural gas drilling had further devastated the country's water reservoirs since Gilboa.

Eol would guarantee that US space endeavors were not upstaged by the mysterious Chinese program. In addition, this would maintain SLS in the country's rocket arsenal and provide for the thousands of contractors that depended on the rocket in business—at least this was the argument of the congressional subcommittee. Many in Congress wanted the funding diverted to clean up America's water supplies.

ESA, the European Space Agency, needed a program promotion too. Its Ariane V rocket could no longer compete with industrial rivals, and its newer Ariane VI, despite its lower pound-to-orbit cost, could not transport heavy payloads into space. ESA needed a new, ambitious project after the ExoMars lander debacles led to a complete reorganization of the agency. *Eol* was to fill this void for ESA. The leadership of ESA approved its participation in 2025 and promised almost three billion Euros, backed by Brussels. A European 'Marshall plan' was in preparation due to the recent political and economic crises threatening the Eurozone, and ESA convinced Brussels that *Eol* should be included in its new allocation.

"Imagine flying in *Eol*," dreamed Manchester, "It would be like our training in *Sea Orb*, remember? It was way more comfortable than Station. I fondly recollect the big windows stretching from floor to ceiling in the common area, in addition to the one in my private quarters."

"Don't remind me," Cousteau chimed in, "I long imagined that *Sea Orb*' was where I wanted to live for the rest of my life. I was actually doing my own science. Now Houston tells me what to do."

Clément Cousteau, born in the small town of Saint-Julien-en-Borne in the Landes department of Southwestern France, always had a lust for exploration. As a boy, he often climbed to the top of the black and white lighthouse in Contis Plage and stared at the ocean through his worn binoculars. He had met his prominent great-grandfather, Jacques-Yves, only a few times. Nonetheless, it was in those brief moments when Jacques-Yves Cousteau was not sharing the oceans onboard his *Calypso* with the rest of the world, that Clément's devotion to the preservation of oceanic life took hold. At the age of six, Clément and his father Marc went to meet the *Calypso* as she docked in Marseilles, France. Jacques-Yves, with his red beanie and harshly wrinkled face leaned on the starboard railing, his eyes fixed to infinity. His tense frown revealed anxious thoughts, until the words, "Grand Papa, Grand Papa," reached his ears and a broad smile lit his face as he noticed young Clément waving his arms.

The *Sea Orbiter II*, nicknamed *Sea Orb'* by its resident crew, was a new exploration vessel, a larger version of the original *Sea Orbiter*, built by French naval architect Jacques Rougerie. *Sea Orbiter II* closely resembled the design of the original and—given ten times the budget—became a workhorse oceanic laboratory. Clément Cousteau was the recipient of the prestigious Piccard Exploration Fellowship, named after the famed Swiss oceanographer. After completing his doctoral work in oceanic microbiology at Woods Hole Oceanographic Institute, Cousteau became a resident scientist on board *Sea Orbiter II*.

"Yes, I remember," longed Williams, "*Sea Orb'* explored our oceans in the same way *Eol* will hopefully explore our solar system," she said. "Long duration missions with a diverse crew of engineers, scientists, and support crew capable of partial self-sustainment, *Sea Orb'* had the true exploration mindset."

"Yes. It was built and designed to be as decoupled from politics as possible, the way ambitious scientific expeditions should always be," asserted Manchester. "I wonder if *Eol* will benefit from the same EfSI status as *Sea Orb'* did?" His question hung in the air.

The 'Expedition for Scientific Inquiry', EfSI, was a charter developed by the United Nations to fundraise for scientific purposes independent of electoral cycles. The idea was to allow bold, international, long-term scientific research programs to operate independently from political uncertainties. These programs were to be funded by an additional overhead on existing UN membership fees. *Sea Orbiter II* was the first beneficiary.

Ignoring Manchester's question, Cousteau said elatedly, "There was nothing else on television."

"*Eol* has been on EfSI money since 2025, Doug," sighed Williams, but she perked up, "Do you remember the helicopter ride that took us to *Sea Orb*'? We were both on our way to explore the undersea Axial volcano on the Juan de Fuca ridge."

"How can I forget that trip…" trailed Manchester as he rubbed his arm clearly bothered by his thoughts. He cheered up almost instantly and continued, "Yeah, the weather was horrid when we left Astoria in Oregon, but it cleared up as we reached *Sea Orbiter II*. What a sight."

Standing forty meters high, and another twenty meters below sea level, *Sea Orbiter II* was shaped like a majestic swan standing on an underwater saucer. That saucer, eighty-five meters in diameter and twelve meters high, could rise to the surface, raising the 'eye' almost sixty meters above sea level. However, during most mission profiles, standard configuration kept the saucer submerged. At the base of the saucer was a bay housing the tethered Robotically Operated Vehicle, *Tethys*, which could reach the bottom of the Mariana trench, over twelve kilometers below. Inside the bay, *Tethys* could be swapped with Deep Submergence Vehicle, *Pytheas*, which could explore the ocean floor untethered to a depth of eight kilometers. With both ROV *Tethys* and DSV *Pytheas*, *Sea Orbiter II* could study the entire water column, from the photic zone, the layer where sunlight penetrates, all the way to the great abysses formed by the bending of our planet's great tectonic plates.

Williams was still recollecting her days on *Sea Orbiter II* when an alarm rang.

"Uh oh," said Manchester reacting to the all-too-familiar sound, "It's that darn ammonia pump again. Why didn't NASA send us up with a spare? I could have used one more space walk."

"ISS this is Houston, code yellow, the ammonia pump went down again."

"Bravo, Sherlock," muttered Cousteau.

"Doug, just turn the pump off manually. We can add the ammonia pump to the list of things that we won't do tomorrow as we turn off the lights," instructed Williams, with slight frustration. "Can you debrief Houston on the incident once you secure it?"

"Aye aye, Captain," saluted Manchester with a

smile. Williams shook her head as she pushed herself off the instrument racks and towards the Cupola, her hands by her side, and drifted headfirst down the module.

Williams loved the Cupola. This was her favorite place on Station. "Now that's a sight I'm going to miss," she thought. She habitually floated towards the center-most window of the Cupola and touched it with the tip of her nose. She then stabilized herself while weightless, and gazed. From here, she felt free, flying above the Earth, absorbing the grandeur of the blue marble that seemed so still, so calm. Night had already fallen at home. Earth glistened with millions of familiar lights as she grazed over the planet at five miles per second. Below her, the vagary and hustle of billions of lives, from the pens of thinkers to the cries of weepers, continued unaware of her watchful eye. "The Black Sea is appropriately named," she thought, as the extreme blackness of the waters contrasted the pale speckled land. Like a bonfire, Tbilissi's lights appeared in the distance. Soon, it was Baku's as she moved from Georgia to Azerbaijan at the speed of a bullet. Blackness swept back as ISS passed over the Caspian Sea. In a few minutes, she would fly over her home country, India, and even spy the lights of Kolkata as they spilled on either side of the Hooghly for miles on-end. Chinsurah was likely there, a small flicker drowned in Kolkata's explosion of light. Lost in this intensity, Jalan Khan, her father, was lighting a candle by the statue of Shiva, praying for his long-lost daughter.

She recalled the icy waters of the Hooghly River that rushed near her home. Built from scraps of bamboo from her uncle's nearby renovation project, and tied together with ropes she found at the fish market, she gripped the structure with all her might as the morning waters snatched her raft away from the shores. She had constructed it in secret, gritting her teeth as her muscles moved beneath the bruises left by her abuser. The raft barely kept her head above the muddy waters while she was powerfully carried by the mighty Himalayan waters that fed over five million people downstream. Limp, drenched, frozen, and barely clinging on to her once buoyant platform, she was pulled out of the waters by the strong arms of the monks at the Belur Math Mission, who were bathing after their prayers. Belur, a sanctuary of wisdom and peace, became her home for the next six years.

"Ain't this a sight," murmured Manchester as the Indian subcontinent unraveled below them.

"You scared me, Doug," she said, her thoughts dissipating. She sighed softly, "Yes, I can't get enough of it," while returning her eyes towards the windows.

They hovered in silence.

"If you saw this for the first time, you'd be hard-pressed to think of all the hardships that are consuming this world. Altitude hides misery."

"Consuming the people of this world," Manchester corrected her. "The planet will be just fine. It has seen worse over the eons. The calamities our planet currently faces are really calamities that threaten our own existence." A silence filled the room as Williams acknowledged his reasoning.

"Do you think we're alone?" she asked a moment later gesturing to above the curved horizon, where the blackness of space was dotted with the Earth's solar neighbors. "Most of these stars have planets," she added. "It really makes you think."

"You know my answer, Sonali," smiled Manchester. "In the universe, I don't think we're alone, but within the reach of humankind, I believe we are. I'm reminded of Arthur C. Clarke's statement… it is a terrifying thought if we are alone in this vastness…"

"…and equally terrifying if we are not alone. Yes, I like the way Clarke wrote," Williams finished.

"If *Eol* is successful," continued Williams, "we are about to embark on a great journey of exploration and discovery. Are we mature enough as a civilization for this? To respectfully explore other worlds and their potential inhabitants, even if they are just microbes?" The vastness of space often filled her with profound questions.

"I think the real question is not about whether humanity is mature enough for exploration, but whether we are mature enough to be the guardians of life if we are alone and do not find life elsewhere," replied Manchester.

Before Williams could answer, Manchester continued, "I came to grab you, we need to be in the airlock in ten minutes to begin campout procedures."

"Right," she responded, "Let's go."

A glitter on the horizon caught her eye, as the terminator—the sunrise line—appeared on Earth's curved horizon.

"That's *Tiangong-3*. It's almost complete," anticipated Manchester.

"The Chinese claimed they would consider an international crew, but so far, nothing," lamented Williams. "Its full capabilities have not been divulged to my knowledge. That will need to happen first before they let any non-Chinese on board, so don't expect it anytime soon."

Campout is a routine procedure on ISS prior to any extravehicular activity, or EVA. The goal is to purge the body of nitrogen over the course of a sleep cycle to avoid decompression sickness. 'The bends' happens when blood vessels clog due to nitrogen gas bubbles coming out of solution due to the sudden lowered pressure. It is known to be excruciatingly painful—and deadly.

"Alright, Clem," said Manchester from within the *Quest* airlock, "We're ready in here."

The *Quest* module is the ISS 'front door' together with the Russian *Pirs* module. To prepare them for the low-pressure of the space-suit, Williams and Manchester spent several hours there, during which the airlock pressure was reduced from the normal 14.7 psi to 10.2 psi. Astronauts 'camp-out' in the airlock prior to an EVA in order to save adaptation time. In their space-suit, the pressure is 5 psi of pure oxygen.

"What happens when you open a bottle of soda?" asked Manchester excitedly into the camera, which was connected live to many classrooms across the world. "By opening the cap, you release the pressure inside the bottle. All the gas that was dissolved inside the liquid now has room to come out of solution and become gas bubbles. That's why we need space suits. It's more than a source of oxygen, it maintains some pressure around the body so that the gas in our blood doesn't form bubbles. That would be very painful," he observed, "We keep the pressure of the suit low to reduce the strain on the material, since the pressure of space is zero."

"He's so good at this," beamed Williams as she zoomed the camera to better capture the soda bottle he clutched in his hands.

"I can't believe we're going to do this," lamented Williams as Manchester helped her suit the Extra-vehicular Mobility Unit, or EMU.

"Do not think of it as the end of an era, but the beginning of a new one," replied Manchester.

"You're so corny, but I like the optimism, Doug,"

Williams smiled.

Click. "Ok, *parfait*," sang Cousteau over the radio. "You both are all set. I'm bringing Canadarm to the hatch."

"Sounds good, Clem', here we go. Ready, Doug?" said Williams.

"Aye," echoed Manchester behind her.

She opened the hatch and shoved the door out of the way. The sight took her breath away. Below her, Earth. She recalled looking out from the upper balcony of the Belur Math temple all these years ago. Forty feet below her perch, she could see the monks by the Hooghly River, like ants by a water rivulet flowing down from the drinking fountain. She remembered holding the rusty railings tightly, priestess Arshana Rai, her mentor, by her side. She had never been so high above the ground.

Now, the ground was not forty feet below her, but over one hundred and fifty miles. As she pushed herself outside, she kept breathing in. No gravity pulled her down. She was falling, and yet she wasn't—the centrifugal force caused by her immense orbital speed canceling the pull of Earth. As she glided out, in silence, the blue planet was all she could see. The white, pervasive brush-strokes of clouds blurred the blue canvas of the oceans with the russet lines of the South American coast revealing a glamorous masterpiece. Suspended in a sunbeam, she finally exhaled as she turned around to see Doug exiting the Station. Her speakers suddenly screeched—it was Doug.

"Perks of the job, eh?" he said.

She smiled back.

"Yes. Let's get to work." They made their way to the *Zvezda-Unity* linkage with the help of Cousteau at the controls of Canadarm.

"Houston, the ROS is detached," said Williams. "The International Space Station is no longer international," she added in a sorrowful voice. One hundred and fifty miles below her, street vendors in Mountain View, California, were busily setting up their vegetable and fruit stalls as the farmer's market opened, unaware that above their heads humankind had begun a new chapter.

"That quote will make the headline of the *New York Times*," asserted Doug. She didn't reply. Although she valued Doug a great deal, she found his enthusiasm excessive at times.

"Good work, Sonali and Doug," came the reply from ground control. Within a few seconds, Williams and Manchester confirmed the firing of thrusters that slowly propelled the ROS away from the American segment of the ISS. In a few months—in theory—the segment would become the backbone of *Eol*.

As she watched ROS move away, she was draped with a silky blanket of melancholy. Her facial expression was still bearing these feelings as she removed her helmet safely back in the hatch.

"What's wrong?" asked Manchester.

"I'm not sure—I feel strange," she paused, "I joined the space program partly to follow the vision of international solidarity I thought space would herald. On my first flight onboard ISS, our crew had combined roots from six continents, and we were doing science, with Principal Investigators from five different countries spanning three continents. It was then that I first truly felt like a citizen of Earth."

Manchester knew better than to interrupt her.

She continued, "Today, I feel that I contributed to making space the least international it has ever been. There are three separate laboratories now, soon only two. Is this really progress? And the remaining won't be joining forces any time soon. How can humanity legitimately explore space with such blatant nationalistic ambitions? We need to be working on the philosophy of space exploration as hard as we are on the engineering."

"I understand how you feel," Manchester replied in a rare gesture of empathy. "But we'll get there. Sometimes one must take a step back to allow the next step forward." He hovered quietly, pondering his statement. "*Eol* will lead the way."

"You have more confidence in *Eol* than I do," she replied sternly. "The financial priorities of the world have shifted considerably from when *Eol* was originally conceived. I was there with Lucia in 2025 at the UN headquarters for its unveiling, and ironically, at the onset of the New York City watershed catastrophe." She shook her head, "No, Doug. Space exploration has changed. Exploration ethics will be displaced by exploration profits, if exploration happens at all."

"It will," Manchester whispered. "Have faith in humanity."

Outside, ATV *Kelvin* was docked.

Ignition awaiting.

FIRST CONTACT

Armando Azua-Bustos

It was time to depart.

He had been chosen by his comrades for the long trip, which would be filled with many, *many* risks.

They trusted him, and he would answer to that trust until the last consequences.

He could see the smiles in their faces… the nods of approval… the small conversations among them reaffirming the decision made.

The rocket was not far from him, if you could still call it 'a rocket,' as it really had an indescribable shape. Only its monstrous engines could be distinguished at the distance.

He started walking towards it. A lonely figure in the starless night, which, against all appearances, was carrying the hopes of an entire planet.

He thought of all the people and belongings he was leaving behind. He thought of the uncertainty of the future… his future… their future.

He comforted himself by thinking that this particular future was as uncertain as any other future.

He did not feel fear anymore, if he ever felt any.

He only had to accomplish his mission.

Without knowing it, the trip to this distant 'Earth' had already started.

THE MARTIAN COUPLE

Dimitra Atri

It was an exciting sol: another batch of astronauts had just landed. Tara and Mir headed to Building 4 where they met Jin, their mentee, who had only landed a few hours ago and was then receiving some much-needed medical attention. Lying in a large bed with numerous tubes penetrating his body, surrounded by instruments closely monitoring his vital signs, his body and mind were both in a state of shock. Jin longed for familiar faces. He had to try very hard to carry on a normal conversation through all the medication, but he was very excited to meet his mentors with whom he had corresponded for over a year.

Mir: "Welcome to Mars."

Tara: "How are you feeling, Jin?"

Jin, with a lot of effort: "Great. It is so good to finally meet you guys."

Tara: "We are so excited you are finally here."

Jin: "I can't believe I'm here. The landing was the most exciting thing since the launch almost a year ago. All I can think about is exploring, going out and running around, but I guess I have to spend some time acclimatizing first."

Mir: "Yeah, you know the drill. You have been in zero gravity for a while now and your body is still adjusting to Martian gravity. You will be surrounded by the medical team for a while, and you need to rest. We'll visit you every day to see how you're coming along. If all goes well, you'll be ready to go within a week."

Jin, with teary eyes: "Thank you for coming here, guys. I don't have words to express myself."

Tara: "We understand. We've both been there."

Jin had been thinking about this conversation all along. What would happen when he landed on Mars? How would he feel? What would his first moments be like? What would he say to his mentors? He felt like he should probably say something profound.

Jin: "You know what I feel? Staying away from Earth gives you a bigger perspective. Mars makes you feel like an Earthling. You can't get that feeling back on Earth."

Mir: "We know. And you are going to discover so many new things here. You should now rest your vocal cords, and try and get some sleep. The doctors will take good care of you, but you need to be patient. Later, you'll walk, run, explore—get to do pretty much whatever you want."

They gave Jin some more tips on acclimatizing to Mars and dealing with all the medications and anxiety. Then, the doctors walked in to monitor his progress.

Tara: "Just text us if you need any help—like you've been doing all along. Take care."

Jin: "Thanks guys. See you tomorrow."

Mir: "You mean solmorrow."

They all laughed. Tara and Mir left Jin to take rest and walked towards Building 19 where they lived.

Over the years, the quality of life on Mars has improved considerably. Their building, like those around it, functioned independently. Enclosed inside thick walls to protect its inhabitants from radiation were residences, offices, gymnasiums, farms, and a huge printer array and chemistry modules to manufacture everyday objects, such as toothbrushes, soap, and shampoo. The large socio-cultural space was not so much a requirement for survival as a social necessity to keep the dwellers sane. All buildings were connected via tunnels, and the entire colony was surrounded by a vast array of solar panels, carefully constructed over a period of decades. The nuclear reactors are stationed far away for safety.

The communal spaces formed the lifeline for most on Mars. People ate all their meals together there and socialized, watched movies, and competed in daily sports competitions.

Tara was from the Pioneer 1 mission, where astronauts signed up for a one-way mission to Mars. It was the first mission where astronauts safely landed on the Martian surface. At first, the thought of never returning to the Earth sounded scary, but true explorers see an unprecedented opportunity beyond fear. Their objective was to use existing robotics available on the Martian surface to construct the first International Martian Station and create a sustainable, habitable environment for humans. Several missions followed, and, over time, a safe, comfortable, and sustainable human complex was built as a result.

They were an unusual couple. Tara was born and raised in a very poor family in Lawrence, Kansas. After graduating from Free State School, she received several scholarships and a free ride at the University of Kansas, where she quickly developed an interest in biology. Her research led her to work in a lab studying the impact of different physical and chemical environments on plant growth. She was encouraged to pursue her PhD at another school, but Tara decided to stay at KU for her graduate studies to remain close to her ailing grandparents.

Mir, the son of an Austrian diplomat, was born in St. Petersburg, and accompanied his father on various diplomatic assignments around the world. They later moved to Mumbai, India where he spent several years of his childhood before moving to Richmond, Virginia. Mir's parents wanted him to develop a global outlook on life like they had, and so Mir went to college at the University of Innsbruck in Austria and got a Masters in Space Sciences from Strasbourg in France. He got another Masters in Computer Science from Virginia Tech. Along with his classmates, he started a small company developing smartphone applications to operate cheap commercial drones. They later moved the company to Mountain View, CA where Mir did some projects with spaceflight engineers. He had worked in the field ever since.

Mir lived with Tara in a tiny studio apartment, like those in East Asian metropolitan areas, bigger than the capsule hotels but smaller than most standard living spaces. Years of research went into designing the perfect living space on Mars. It had to be uniform for all astronauts, be comfortable enough for long-term living, and be built keeping the limited resources available on the planet in mind. The result was a small studio apartment, which could be customized based on individual needs. There was enough space to house a queen size bed, a small couch, two reclining chairs but not enough space to play or walk around.

A couple of sols later, after Jin recovered and acclimatized to Martian conditions, he went up to Tara and Mir's apartment one evening. They were watching Seinfeld while Mir prepared drinks. They had a wide selection already loaded into the tap, as it was called. It was similar to a gas station coffee machine, except the variety was nearly infinite.

Mir: "I'm going with Malbec, what do you guys want?"

Tara: "No wine for me Mr. Fancy Pants, get me a beer. I'll go with wheat state golden." She said jokingly. They all laughed. It was a local beer from Lawrence, where she spent much of her life.

Jin: "I'll go with Shanghai Mijiu—you should have it there". They laughed again. Shanghai Mijiu was a popular wine among college students in China.

Mir and Tara were on the couch, while Jin reclined in a chair.

Jin: "So, how is it living here? I mean you have been living here for years now, do you guys like it?" He asked to start a conversation.

Mir: "For someone who hasn't experienced it first-hand, it is difficult to express how I feel living here. For someone on Earth, I give the standard answer: Since the surface gravity is too small, you have this weird feeling all the time. Imagine yourself on a roller coaster ride, when you are falling, you get an unusual feeling in your gut. Imagine feeling that all the time. We are falling all the time, and for years. There are several problems which one has to deal with while living here. One has to take a variety of medicine to counter the changes in your body and mind, and they all have side effects. We were all aware of the consequences, but I couldn't have anticipated the reality. We exercise everyday to survive in this extremely harsh yet surprisingly comfortable environment."

Tara: "We make use of natural light as much as possible, which itself is less than half of what you get on the Earth. Blah blah…"

Mir: "But in reality you get used to everything with time, and things become stable in your body and mind. Life is very simple here. You have everything that you need, but not necessarily everything you want. There is no end to things one wants."

"At any time, we are seconds away from disaster and depend on each other for our survival and well being. I guess that's what makes us a tightly knit community, and the depth of conversations we have here is rare back home."

Tara: "It is interesting to see how the meaning of home changes with place. Who knew instead of a city, state, country or continent, you'd be calling a planet as a 'home.' I mean, sure, we all know it is where we live, but we generally are more specific when we talk about home."

Meanwhile on TV:

Jerry: "My idea of the perfect living room would be the bridge on the Starship Enterprise. You know what I mean? Big chair, nice screen, remote control. That's why Star Trek really was the ultimate male fantasy. Just hurling through space in your living room, watching TV. That's why all the aliens were always dropping in, because Kirk was the only one that had a big screen. They came over Friday night, Klingon boxing... gotta be there."

Jin: "So, how did you guys meet?"

Tara: "I came here before Mir. He was my mentee. We started working together on some projects and became close. It has been 4 years now, I guess, but it seems such a long time ago," she reminisced.

Mir: "I already liked her back home, and I wished so badly for them to assign me to her as a mentor," they laughed.

Mir: "Tell us your story, Jin. Do you have a girlfriend?"

Jin: "I'm actually married. My wife was pregnant when I left home, and we had a baby girl while I was in transit."

Tara: "Wow, congratulations. You are so young,

and we never would have guessed you had a family to take care of back home," she said with enthusiasm.

Jin: "Yeah, we married early. It was difficult to leave them for a couple of years and come here. But I never could have lived with the fact that I had the opportunity to visit Mars and missed it. So we decided that it would be best if I pursue my dream and start a normal family life again once I'm back home."

Mir: "What do you mean, a couple of years? I am sorry to bring this up, but you know that we don't have the technology yet, don't you?" he asked looking puzzled.

Jin: "You mean you don't know about the Pico project at CERN? They are in the final stages of building the capacitor. They probably already have it built by now." He responded with amusement.

It was a tough problem to crack. Only a few years ago, the solution seemed impossible to fathom. The source of all energy on Mars is solar and nuclear. All the energy harnessed by the vast array of solar panels was stored in batteries. With the existing setup, the charge wasn't enough to generate the heat required to initiate a controlled chain reaction. Mars didn't yet have the power to fuel the nuclear engines and escape the gravitational field. Transporting humans back to the Earth had remained a distant dream.

They had worked on that project together back home. Mir brought his expertise in physics, and his technological skill, to develop computer algorithms that solved complex equations. Tara brought her expertise in circuitry and building fully-functional devices. The solution was right there. If the energy was released from a capacitor in a picosecond, it would produce enough heat to initiate the reactions. But how would one design such a capacitor? It was a physics problem. Over the years they've worked together on Mars, they worked alongside numerous collaborators on Earth and tried to come up with a design, and although it didn't quite provide the required charge, they were close. A prototype design was sent to Earth so that it will be tested and perfected and a replica will be launched. If it worked, the parts would be printed on Mars, assembled, and ready to go. At least that was the plan they were aware of.

Tara: "We've been hearing about that for years. We used to receive memos once every couple of weeks about it, but nothing worked out. In fact, Mir was on the first mission where they were promised a trip back within a year. They were shown a prototype technology which would enable them to go back, but it never succeeded. You shouldn't take them seriously until they have something to demonstrate."

Mir: "I follow the research in this area very closely and am in touch with colleagues at CERN. Sorry to break your heart, but I'll be the first to know if such a thing happens."

Jin: "I can understand your skepticism, but they have already built a prototype engine on a smaller scale."

Mir: "I heard rumors about that years ago, but you still shouldn't take them seriously."

Jin: "I assure you, these are not rumors. Our batch of astronauts went to Nevada, where the engine was assembled and tested. We saw the test ourselves, and we studied the performance data very carefully. They told us to maintain confidentiality or face consequences. Only my wife knows, because without that assurance I wouldn't have come here. The secret is safe with her because she keeps her distance from the media and is not active on social media, either."

Mir: "If this were true, shouldn't we be the first people to get this news?" He was worried.

Jin: "I also wondered that, but then they told us how such news can leak to the media, potentially embarrassing the agencies yet again. Do you remember how one of the former astronauts sent a message to his family hinting that he might be back? After it circulated on social media, it ended up on television sets around the globe."

Tara: "True, but we have strict regulations about that now, and we are all very careful with that. Mir, do you want to ask Sachin what's going on?" She was worried too.

Sachin was their colleague who came with Mir and was responsible for the assembly and testing of spacecraft engines.

Mir: "I'm going to write to Savannah and Felix directly. Sachin might not be able to give us anything. You know how he is. They should be able to tell whether it is just a PR for new recruits, or if there is something serious about it."

Savannah: I am hearing news about the pico project. Is there something I should know

about? —Mir

Felix: I am hearing about the tests at the Nevada facility. Is there something I should know about? —Mir

After Jin went back to his place, Tara and Mir became restless, eagerly awaiting a response from Savannah or Felix. There is an expected delay of several minutes in any kind of communication with the Earth, but even knowing that didn't help their anxiety. Tara went to take a shower while Mir kept pacing the room. They were dealing with stress in their own ways. After waiting for two long hours, they decided to go to bed. They couldn't sleep.

It was an unusual morning. Typically while preparing breakfast together, they shared stories of their childhood, friends, and family before leaving for work. Today, there were no words, no eye contact. They both knew what they had done. The silence was deafening.

Mir knew what was happening to Tara. All of a sudden, Tara began to cry. Mir expected it, but neither of them knew how to handle the situation.

Tara: "What will happen to us?" she exclaimed loudly.

Mir kept quiet. He took a sip of his coffee and looked at a distance outside the window.

Tara: "Are you going to leave me and go?"

Mir, taking a deep breath in a serious tone: "You need to trust me. I need some time to think. There is a lot going on in my head right now."

Tara left the room. Mir didn't feel like it, but finished his breakfast quietly. His entire life was now flashing in front of him.

Things have changed over the years. When I was new here, I was on cloud nine, on the biggest adventure of my life. I would send and receive tons of video messages from family and friends everyday. Then things became routine here, and I had nothing new to say. There was a phase when I desperately wanted to get back to Earth. I missed everything about the Earth. No matter how comfortable and communal the environment we have created on Mars, it is artificial. I often wonder whether I am an explorer, as I imagine myself to be, or just a couch potato on Mars?

I got over that phase too, and liked living here just like most people do. Back home, friends now have real jobs, families with kids, and suburban houses with minivans, stocks, and lawnmowers. I, on the other hand, am still figuring out what to do with my life. But I have made great friends here, and we live together like a big family. And most importantly, I have Tara. Why would I go back?

It is very peaceful here, and we can carry on with our lives without any distractions or social pressures. We have made some very close friends here, which might be difficult to do once we are back home.

We are going to be together wherever we are. I often wonder whether we have become Martians? Do we belong to the Earth? Can we have a life together here forever?

THE LITTLEST DUCKLING

Jacob Haqq-Misra

Gracie arrived on Mars two hours after the Osiris mat was discovered. Both were placed in quarantine, while Commander Abrams consulted with his staff.

"Just over three kilograms, and forty-five centimeters long," reported Ensign Smith. "Mother is well, and baby is stable."

"And the condition?"

"A severe combined immunodeficiency as well as respiratory defects. Most likely genetic."

"Prognosis?"

"Fatal, a few months at best." Smith frowned. "Stem cell transplantation on Earth might save her, but we can do nothing here."

Abrams paced the circumference of his chambers and called upon his Chief Scientist. "Max, how long can Osiris survive on its own?"

"The mat lost its habitat because of the polar ice harvest," explained Max, "and it has dwindled to the brink of extinction. We can help it survive with our technology, but we must decide soon. Osiris can only withstand a few more nights before it vanishes."

"What would it cost?"

"We need a mobile environmental shelter to protect Osiris, drawing at least ten kilowatts from the fission grid," said Max, "plus two microbiologists on site."

"And Gracie?"

"Fifteen kilowatts to keep her breathing and isolated," said Smith. "Power has already been cut from the vegetable garden and all research stations."

Abrams let out a deep and bellowing sigh. "Thirty seven kilowatts," he said, beckoning to his Chief Engineer for an approving nod, "is all the power we have. I need fourteen just to keep the cabin from imploding and another eight to feed our crew of thirty. We cannot save them both."

A passing murmur of uneasiness was interrupted by Max's candor. "Osiris is dying because of us, and it will die without us," he asserted, "but Gracie will perish no matter what we do."

"And what of Gracie's parents?"

"I mourn for their loss," said Max, "but her condition is fatal. Prolonging Gracie's life means we lose both her and Osiris."

"Would you suggest the same if Gracie were yours?"

Max nodded. "The Osiris mat is the first extraterrestrial life we have discovered. We cannot risk its loss."

"And Gracie is the first infant to be born in space," offered Smith. "Her legacy deserves better and obligates us to try."

"On Earth, I would agree with you," replied Max, "but our resources are limited here. We are biological creatures, and the perilous pressures of selection always lay claim to the weaklings, the runts, and the littlest ducklings. On a station like ours, we cannot fight nature without risking our own survival."

Abrams stepped to the door and faced his staff. "Our mission is to explore," he said, "but our allegiance is to our fellow human beings. I will mourn the loss of Osiris, but my conscience would forever roam restless if we abandoned one of our own. We are indeed creatures of biology, and it is our instinct for compassion that makes us truly human."

THE PARTY AT THE END OF THE WORLD

Seth D. Baum

December 31st, five billion years from now

Every year since the rise of global human civilization, people on Earth have celebrated New Year's Eve—once a year for over five billion years. Customs have changed, the species has dramatically evolved, but the New Year's tradition has stayed intact. Another lap around the Sun. It never loses significance, not for the hardy few who have remained on the home planet all these years, these long, glorious years.

This year is different. This is it. The end of the world. The last party on Earth. In just two days, it will become physically impossible to live on Earth. Our orbiting sunshades will no longer be able to keep out the warming rays of the Sun. Without the sunshades, Earth would have become uninhabitable billions of years ago. In fact, most planets would have died out long ago. But Earth is not most planets. Earth is home. For two more days.

It boggles the mind to think that the entire civilized population of the multiverse once lived right here. All on one little planet. A beautiful planet, for sure, but still, just one little planet. Of course, the civilized population was tiny back then, just a few billion. Today's population wouldn't even fit on a few billion Earths. That's what billions of years of cosmic expansion will do. Those early humans did get one thing right—it is a small world after all.

It's crazy to think that we almost didn't make it. Yet here we are, stretched across countless galaxies, using most of their energy to power our lives. We'll surely outlive the stars. But we almost failed to outlive our own immaturity. That would have been horrible. Beyond horrible. A sleeping universe, with no one to appreciate its beauty, no one to explore it, no one to make the most of life. Completely worthless.

That is why we are celebrating on Earth tonight. We are celebrating our existence. Our blessed, beautiful existence. Without it, we would be nothing. Literally, nothing. We are celebrating quite simply because we can. Right here on Earth, right where it all started. One last time.

Some people say it's selfish to celebrate our own existence. Not me. I don't believe that one bit. They say we should be celebrating the stars that fuel us, or the planets we stand on, or the gravity that keeps us from floating away. Yeah, sure, those all matter. But we're why those things matter. We're what brings them to life. Celebrating our existence forces us to remember that.

Celebrating our existence also forces us to pay homage to those who made our existence possible. Our parents, of course. And our grandparents, and all our ancestors before them. They are why we are alive. Above all, we pay homage to the Heroes. Without them, there would be no ancestors.

The Age of Heroes was the turning point. Early civilization was almost destroyed by its own immaturity. The Age of Heroes was when we started to mature. The ship of civilization was sailing on the wrong course. During the Age of Heroes, we set it right. All our successes, all the cosmic marvels we've achieved—they all started there.

The Heroes are our legends. They represent our highest ideals and aspirations. They had so little, compared to us, yet they accomplished so much more. Ever since the Age of Heroes, many of us have tried to be great. Some of us even succeeded. But try as we might, no one can be as great as them. They had the most important job in the history of civilization, no, in the history of the universe. And they succeeded.

We all know, it was a scary close call. The Heroes got off to a slow start. It took them a long time to recognize their mission. Almost too long. And some of them didn't accept it, at least not at first. It's no wonder why. I wouldn't want so much responsibility. I mean, I would, but I wouldn't want it to sneak up on me like that. Everyone today has careful training for their work, honed from billions of years of experience. The Heroes had to figure it out as they went, for a mission no one told them they had. No wonder it was a close call.

But they made it. They recognized what they were up against, they stepped up to the challenge, and they made it. We made it. Civilization made it. Once and for all. Right here on Earth. The home planet. Where it all started. That's quite a lot to celebrate. One last time.

The party preparations are all set. Actually, we've been planning this party for a few million years, when the sunshades started thinning. Those sunshades have been rebuilt and repaired so many times, we almost thought they'd last forever. But no sunshade lasts forever. Not even on Earth.

I still think we could have tacked on a few more patches to keep the sunshade going. I believe this sacred planet could still take us a few more laps around the Sun, if we really wanted. But the ride has to end eventually. We might as well end it now. And end it in style.

It's easy to celebrate a planet. You can tune into its highlight reel and bask in its greatest moments. You can dance the night away to its best music, if you enjoy wearing legs. But those things you can do from anywhere. Me, I like to lie flat on the ground, letting the planet's seismic vibrations massage my body as I admire its view of its galaxy. That, you can only do if you're on the planet. That's how I'm spending my last day on Earth.

Tomorrow, we hop in our ships and head out before the sunshades break. A lot of people are going to Mars or Titan. I'm going to wander the galaxy for a while, try to find somewhere else I fit in. Not sure where that would be.

A few people decided not to bother. They're going down with the ship, staying here on Earth to die. So be it. But that's tomorrow.

Tonight, we party.

SANTA

Armando Azua-Bustos

Christmas Eve came in the blink of an eye.

Little Timmy was barely able to sleep that night.

When sleep was finally overcoming him, he heard a soft tinkling of bells and servo motors on the first floor.

Quiet as a terran mouse, he got out of bed and floated to the door, which fortunately, was half closed.

He peered down and, with an almost infinite joy, saw Santa Claus arranging many big gift boxes around the Christmas tree.

He tried to guess how many of these gifts were actually for him.

He wanted to soar down, speak to him, tell him how long he had waited for him... how happy he was by having him in his home.

But he restrained himself. He wanted to enjoy this moment for one more second. He thought of all of the children of his binary system that Santa had still to visit that night.

Then, in another blink of an eye, thousands of little stars exploded all over the living room… and Santa was gone.

This had been, without any doubt, the best night of his life.

STOPPED CLOCK

Zach Adam

"Lips bleed. Lips always bleed out.
I crawl out of my jump.
Living motion, I'm a living trench dug into the
mountainside."

I remember fixing a hatch motor that had jammed, there was a power surge and then I saw an arm lying on the floor. In curiosity, I watched the fingers writhe slightly, wondering whose arm it was and how long I'd failed to notice it there. When I saw that the arm was wearing part of my shirt, I wondered if the fingers were moving because of some latent impulse from my brain, a last flush of electrochemical command. Or whether the power surge had somehow passed along the nerves at the moment of severance, the fingers blindly commanded by the same ship that carries me through the stars.

It wasn't fair.

That was the moment I realized that it was my arm. The same moment that I felt it wasn't fair. Not losing the arm mind you, but not being able to control it any longer. Even in the last moment of its existence as part of an organic creature, with nearly all of its cells still living off of the meals I had eaten and the oxygen I had breathed. I was not in control of my own arm. And it wasn't fair. There's precious little in the universe that we can fool ourselves into pretending that we truly and fully control. Now, the first and most primitive piece of my body that I could control was lying on the floor.

That I was still alive at all was something of a miracle after all of these years. Once, I woke up with a tingling feeling in my ear. A micrometeorite had passed straight through my bunk while I slept, piercing my ear at an oblique angle. It didn't bleed much, might not have even needed a bandage. I estimate that it must have passed through my ear at roughly 30 times the speed of sound, which meant that if I had been awake, I would have heard my own ear being pierced only after the micrometeorite had left the spacecraft altogether and returned to the vacuum of space. Two fragments of stellar history touching one another in the void for an in-

stant—each set in motion long ago by forces neither could fully comprehend.

The departure day was so long ago that I didn't
recall it with clarity. I feel certain that I departed
a world that had many people—that their minds
had shaped my ship, their hands had built it, and
their decisions had placed me within it. But their
faces and the circumstances of departure had long
ago faded from memory. What I know for certain
remains encrypted in the design and contents of
this ship. This was to be a multi-generational ship.
There were many different rooms with personal belongings, food production equipment, and
medical supplies (a large proportion of which were
nursery- or child-related). We traveled away from
the star directly aft of travel direction, and toward
the star forward of travel direction. Many aspects
of the ship's operation and navigation are analog in
design, built into the ship itself, requiring no human intervention to maintain and are thus imper-
vious to the radiation bath we swim through. The
same cannot be said of most of the ship's digital
computers—there are fragments of information of
course, but very little can be reconstructed into a
sensible whole. The ship, like its inhabitant, has be-

come a functional amnesiac.

But the inhabitant, like its ship, is not without utility. What exactly separated me from the others to put me aboard the ship is unclear, but likely can be attributed to my creative use of machines. Many individual devices aboard the ship are still functional, but stay powered-down most of the time. I make great use of them to maintain a symbiotic existence. Most of the time this is simple repair work. But sometimes I manufacture entirely new components to replace those that have become worn out or damaged.

The arm was my first real challenge. I told myself that if I could keep a lumbering spacecraft in good shape as it wandered between the stars, I could surely manage a limb fabrication. The printers on board can process an incredible array of polymers and alloys, so the skeletal shapes, muscle fibers and tendons could be improvised relatively easily. The real challenge was interfacing the prosthetic with the nerve endings at the stump. I eventually settled on a combined bio-mechanical approach, creating microfiberous elastomer tubes that ran the length of the plasticized muscles, which were pre-injected with stem cell tissues from the ship's stores. After rather painfully re-exposing the healing surface, I bonded the prosthetic to my skeleton with a biologically derived epoxy and waited for the stem cells inoculated with nerve bundles to rejoin the truncated nerve endings.

According to the remaining physician's volumes onboard, my immune system was about to kick into overdrive. I steeled myself for days of pain and inflammation as my body would almost certainly reject this clumsy graft as an imposter. Though, that's not what happened—my body effortlessly accepted the attachment. Though it could not provide the sense of touch of the original, I celebrated my successful repair by drinking the whiskey that I'd put aside to self-medicate, using the new arm to lift the delicate amethyst glass to my lips until I passed into a dreamless drunken bliss.

The success of the procedure began to stir some deep, dark feelings in my soul. The stem cells that enabled the grafting operation were on board to ensure the survival of spaceborne children who were certain to develop genetic diseases as their bodies grew in the unfamiliar environment of deep space. The automatic medical scanners had been indicating to me that my immune system had been degrading for many years. This degree of degradation almost certainly explained why my body had accepted the grafting procedure without any hint of inflammation, as it had simply given up fighting off invasions. I was steadily becoming weaker and more easily fatigued. The scanner recommended stem cell therapy as a means of preventing total immunodeficiency. The operation's success was a reminder to me that I had stopped fighting for my own survival. So I refused the stem cell therapy.

I had been alone for years on the ship by that point, and in the midst of my solitude I saw very little reason to survive. For reasons that I cannot fully explain, I had accepted that my time would end, and that I would not stand in the way of natural circumstances. I wouldn't hasten my death, but I wouldn't delay it either.

The loss of my arm, and my desire to repair the loss, exposed and exacerbated a paradox that made me very uncomfortable: I had resolved not to stand in the way of certain death, but I would also readily employ (and celebrate) any medical technique that enabled my continued ability not to stand in the way of death. But how can I possibly divide the whole of my body into essential and non-essential pieces, especially when my survival depended on every part of my bodily functioning? Even as I considered my motivations—and my justifications—the closest I could come to putting it into words was to think that my arm served the ship, but my immune system served only me. By this logic, it was thus expendable where the arm was not. The distinction made no logical sense, but became a very powerful discriminator of my actions. I would certainly die, and the ship wouldn't care or notice when it happened. But if I was required to make a repair to the ship's systems while I was still alive, then pride dictated that I would find a way—no matter the cost.

Using the stem cells from the nursery had also revived a bitter irony. Perhaps the only fragment of my previous self: I had foregone having children to go to space. I can't recall now who I was with, what he was like, or when we separated, but I know that I was forced to decide between dedication to the mission and procreation. I chose the mission. I can't recall if my duty bound me to bear children once aboard the ship. If so, it became moot after the other crewmembers had passed. Perhaps the reason this fragment of my identity didn't degrade after all of these years is that I can imagine and appreciate the humor of a multi-generational ship with no people, kept alive by a sole survivor who chose not to have children to ensure her immortality.

In moments of darkest levity, I imagined that my laughter was transmitted as a minute portion of energy, at the speed of light, to all passing stars. At my current speed, an observer in orbit around one of those stars would see only a still frame of my tortured expression frozen in time.

For a long time after the operation, I gradually reconciled this new knowledge of my peculiar motivations. I don't think the operation itself created the paradox, but the situation forced me to consciously confront something that had always been a part of my self-conception. Circumstances had made that part of my being tragically and critically relevant to my survival. The paradox slowly lumbered back to the recesses of my mind as I faced a steadily increasing spectrum of malfunctions that now required most of my attention. The ship's repairs were manageable, but my own malfunctions were beginning to take on a new level of urgency.

Around the time I lost my arm, I vaguely recollect approaching the end of a typical human lifespan. I don't think I'd noticed how old I was getting until I realized that the only part of my body that didn't ache was my new arm. It moved, bent, and flexed without complaint. While the loss of touch was initially disappointing, I found that my mind more or less imagined the sensory perception anyway, filling in the void and leaving me without want.

Not surprisingly, after years of living on a ship with nothing but drinkable company, my liver was the first part of my body to give out. Creating and printing a suitable synthetic material was challenging enough, but figuring out how to guide the table surgeon while being unconscious for key parts of the procedure required some improvisation. The automated table surgeon instrument suite could handle a basic repertoire of invasive procedures and anesthetic delivery to see the replacement through, but required user inputs at key decision points that were supposed to be administered by a medical doctor to keep the recognition patterns from going off the deep end; a simple yes or no could keep my kidney from being mistaken for my spleen. Using the remote version of the software also required having to physically place the new organ in my body in the middle of the procedure, properly aligned so that the pattern recognition software could locate and tag the position markers to sew me up.

As the anesthetic entered my veins and I lost consciousness, I felt panic. I had reviewed the entire decision tree of the surgery program, and timed the anesthetic program to bring me to near consciousness throughout the surgery to keep the procedure moving forward. I even had a separate display independently programmed to remind me where we were in the process, and to prompt me to make the right decision in the haze of an impaired state.

I felt panic, because if there was an offset in the timing of revival by as little as ten minutes, or if I failed to follow the cues in the prompt program, I might not wake up at all, or worse yet, I might wake to a horror show of self-inflicted disembowelment. But the remote surgery solution necessitated a step even riskier than the liver replacement itself. There needed to be a permanent, constant-flow, self-enclosed blood pump as a safeguard against cardiac arrest. It would continue flowing, regardless of the level of psychological or physiological stress that I might encounter.

I don't consciously recall waking up throughout the procedure to guide the automated table surgeon. Occasionally I have very strong dreams where my hands are covered in blood and I am performing a self-dissection. In the middle of my open chest I see organs, teeth, and fragments of bone, but nothing is attached to anything. I clumsily search through everything I find, passing each item to a clean steel pan. In my dreams, I think that I feel the panic that I felt just before going unconscious, but it's a disconnected panic, as though I can only feel it in my legs, eyes, scalp, and skin.

When I did wake up, after all procedures had been completed, I looked down at the stitches across my chest and side and felt relieved. I felt light and unstoppable. From that moment onward, I never again felt panic.

I didn't understand what panic really was until it had left me. Panic is an organic feeling. It comes from an instinctive desire to maintain one's own collection of cells in their current arrangement. A group of one type of cells initiates a physiological response that shakes the entire body to its core, instantly repurposing every cell to this singular end, regardless of its primary function in the body.

In the course of that surgery, I crossed some threshold. My body was now something to maintain, to repair and carry on. I am not sentimental, and I don't recall carrying any particularly strong emotions about the human heart even when I had one. But the pump that hums softly in my chest runs all the time, humming slightly more when I exert myself, but never pounding, never demanding my attention, and never threatening to stop. It doesn't shift into action instantaneously because it's in action continuously. Life pulses—it weakens and thrives in rhythms of its own. I wonder sometimes whether humans are actually accustomed to a pervasive feeling of panic, the spaces between heart beats are a silent death noticeable only in the moment when the next beat fails to materialize.

The moment when I regained consciousness was a rebirth—an anti-birth. Physically, I felt fine, better, in fact, than I had in a long time. The constant fatigue slowly left my body, and I found myself able to carry on more tasks in a given period than was possible before. I don't recall the order of subsequent surgeries that followed, but replacements became routine. Each upgrade lifted a burden from the failing remainder of my body. And I felt much younger than before.

The loss of pervasive panic also brought with it the unexpected loss of the sense of time's passing. Months and years became years and decades that trailed off into an untillable soil. There is no daily cycle on this ship, just the constant glide of space. If there were such a routine, it would be the cycle of maintenance and repair. Yes, ships and machines have their own diurnal patterns. Their own needs and wants become companion personalities, each with its own quirks, processed by the mind that cares for them. My life had truly become shaped to this task. The replacement of filters, draining and filling of tanks, and the regeneration of organic matter became its own workday. I timed it once long ago with an external chronometer, out of curiosity for just how much time passed during my now-typical day, choosing to draw a line for a particular turnover of an organic processing tank used to recover nitrogen fertilizer. I don't recall the exact figure, but it was on the order of dozens of years. The specific number has since lost its visceral meaning to me, as I apparently hadn't been in orbit around a star for centuries. There was no fully organic being left to remind me of a year's significance, and I no longer felt any physical attachment to the span of a life. Even the word 'year', struck me as a word from a foreign tongue, to be memorized in use but not felt in observation.

Indeed, words began to have a diffused meaning for me. Though I travel amongst the stars, my universe has collapsed to the contour of the ship. With the replacement of so many of my internal organs and external appendages over the years, I no longer inhabit a time cycle of my own. The ship and I carry one together. While reviewing some very old maintenance documents, I came across a word that I had to cross-reference in a dictionary: service. The definition confused me for a short time, as I couldn't readily recall if I was servicing the ship or whether the ship was servicing me.

The details of the ship's mission have long since faded and become deformed in my mind. Though the ship's design tells me that it was intended to survive for a very long period of time and with a large number of people, I can't recall why those people left their homes to travel in space. Was it an emergency, or mere relocation?

I had given up trying to recall or determine what that purpose was, until the ship began to decelerate. We were approaching the destination.

I had a slight feeling of emptiness and betrayal that the ship had moved of its own accord without notifying me; I was caught by surprise. It was the first real surprise I'd had in ages. Upon reflection, I realized that there was no way the ship could tell me anything at all, since the integrated digital computers had all fallen prey to entropy during the voyage.

When the ship rotated and began to decelerate, I was resting in a warm bath of water mixed with salts and synthetic fatty acids. With the replacement of all of my outer joints, I found soaking to be much more efficient than lubricating and maintaining the joints separately. At first, I thought that something had malfunctioned, but the smoothness and coordination of the movement was unlike any other errant motions that I had experienced on the ship during previous episodes of disrepair. It was difficult to find a viewing port facing the forward direction that was not cracked, scratched, nicked, corroded, or opaque with great age, but I finally found a suitable patch of window that had been somewhat protected by a large engine cowling. The star in front of us was so close that I could resolve numerous points of light in orbit—planets, no doubt.

The idea of rejoining other people struck me as an outlandishly remote possibility—one I'd stopped considering long ago. Obviously, the ship functioned well enough to sense the approaching system and implement a deceleration trajectory. It may have even been capable of entering orbit around one of the planets on its own. But then what? Except for a few space suits that could be used to make exterior repairs, I had never seen any smaller ships or systems on board capable of carrying people to or from the ship. In the depths of my mind, I couldn't recall what a vehicle should look like that would carry people down to a planet.

I deduced that there must be people and vehicles already in the approaching star system capable of planetary transportation, and that they were probably expecting some kind of communication. At this distance, they may even have powerful radio and visual telescopes locked onto the ship, looking for some kind of answer as to why we had dropped out of communication during the voyage. Though the ship's primary and backup communications systems had long since decayed beyond repair, I wondered if I could use some smaller units aboard that might put me in range of the planet's transmitters. The ship and I were dropping from the near-light speeds at which we'd coasted during the trip, but we were still moving pretty fast. The signal wouldn't reach the system much sooner than when we would arrive ourselves, and the bandwidth would be pretty limited. But a brief message out was certainly possible, even if I was unable to receive a reply.

I spent the next few cycles searching through every emergency supply kit on the ship. I could find no devices specialized for near-light transmission and reception, but I did find three rugged ground-standard radio devices in a surface landing kit of the same make and model. These could be scavenged for parts and design ideas. By this point, my memory regarding electromagnetic physics had become severely compromised by neglect. I was fairly certain that I could retrofit most of the radio components to boost their range using their existing design as a template, but I needed to rebuild much of my knowledge to use the printers on the ship to design and manufacture the right components.

I was, and am still, mute. I was as silent as my voyage through space. I hadn't spoken a word for decades, perhaps centuries. I couldn't recall if my voice had left me for lack of use, or if one of my surgical interventions had taken the power of speech from me inadvertently. It very well could have been either or both. I simply hadn't noticed. Now that I was faced with contact with people, it felt like contact for the first time with an alien civilization. I thought about how bodies made sounds with some combination of their chests, noses, and throats, and how those sounds were of a pitch and intonation that matched elements of their surroundings. My surroundings were the sounds of motors, gears, servos, pumps, and the few digital devices that I could keep running that supported my life, folded neatly into an envelope of darkness.

What would I transmit? There was no logical

start except a systematic description of the health and status of the crew. My first message was:

Attention planetary inhabitants: multigenerational light ship approaching. One survivor and abundant supplies aboard. Arrival calculated in 2.57 Earth-years. Unable to receive radio messages. Survivor and ship are in equilibrium condition.

But in relearning the physics of building the transmitter, I realized that I must rebuild my language skills, my conversations, my expectation of response, and the ability to deliver a message of worth to another being capable of understanding what I had lived, capable of understanding why I was no longer human. The story of how and why I was still alive. I labored over the next message for months, relearning my native language to the level of explanation and exposition. I am transmitting it to you now, so that it may serve as a record of my state of mind, body, and being when we completed our voyage and met your people for the first time. Your escort ships have left two of your planets and are meeting us here as we decelerate for the last time. I am ready to speak again.

In relearning my native language to explain my experience to you, I have recalled groups of words that I had long forgotten: betrayal, alone, fight. These words have carried no meaning for me for centuries, but now that I am rejoining people I realize that I am no longer of people. I realize now that your ships may not welcome my presence. I did not welcome my death, but I did not embrace my life. I traded my life to death, piece by piece, so that I could continue to move forward.

I transmit my story to you now, so that you may know that, whatever I have become across this voyage, and however different I may appear to you, I used to be one of you. There are still parts of my body that may be affected by your native illnesses, so I may not survive meeting you long enough to convey the essence of my existence, or to explain how I survived for so long.

Centuries ago, I made a choice that moved my cells in your direction. This became my priority above all else. It became my purpose above all explanation. It became my reality above all complication. I wish only to see this mission completed, for the small chance that I may finally understand why.

I am no closer to understanding who or what I was before the trip, but I think that I better understand the psychological pressures that allowed me to survive for those millennia. My perception of time has sped up significantly in recent days as I've interacted with more and more fully organic people, and I'm already forgetting the true feeling of symbiosis that I developed with the spacecraft. I am no longer connected to it in the same way, because we no longer rely on one another to continue.

Feelings of affection, appreciation, and modest amounts of empathy have returned to my consciousness. I am thankful that I did not have these feelings when I docked with the approaching ships. The terrified looks on the faces of the doctors and engineers would have caused me extreme discomfort if I had known how to read the nuanced tones and expressions that accompanied their diagnoses. I could not speak, and my human body was estimated to have been replaced with approximately 88% synthetic components by the end of the trip. They had anticipated a human survivor, not a self-created origami project.

One of the first pieces of information that was

conveyed to me was that the inhabitants of this star system were not expecting our ship. Though more fragments of data have been recovered from the ship's ancient computers since my arrival, there is very little evidence of the political or social circumstances that prompted our departure. I tried to recall perceptions that would be helpful, and I tried to review and interpret the recovered data, but with little success. Indeed, even the circumstances of the departure of their own ancestors is a subject of vociferous, ongoing debate.

I am now faced with a difficult decision for the first time that I can recall in centuries. It is difficult because it is entirely optional, and driven only by my own personal preferences without reference to anyone or anything else. Having been relieved of the burden of our passage through space, my priorities have shifted in ways that I find very disorienting. I am anchored on this planet now, but I am tethered only to myself, and perhaps I am less constant than I imagined myself to be.

A doctor began examining me after I arrived, fascinated by my ability to survive and to make the necessary surgical alterations using the automated system. He carefully examined the twelve percent that remained of my organic body, and discovered a small number of ova tucked away in a partially plasticized segment of my reproductive system. Combined with the genetic information in the remainder of my cells, he seems relatively sure that a viable ovum can be produced, and that I may actually be capable of carrying my own child to term using donor organs. This will require replacing a number of my synthetic components with organic organs. I may die in the process, even before having the chance to hold my child.

When I think of refusing the procedure, I feel panic. I am relieved to feel panic once again.

Liked what you read? Stay in touch with us!

Follow us on Twitter: **@BlueMarbleSpace**

Like us on Facebook:
facebook.com/BMSInstituteofScience

Email us: **info@bmsis.org**.

Join SAGANet at **saganet.org** and share
your thoughts about science, philosophy,
fiction, and the future.

ABOUT US

Zach Adam holds a Ph.D. in earth sciences from Montana State University. He lives in Boston, Massachusetts.

Dimitra Atri holds a Ph.D. in physics from the University of Kansas. He lives in Athens, West Virginia.

Armando Azua-Bustos holds a Ph.D. in molecular genetics & microbiology from Pontifica Universidad Católica de Chile. He lives in Santiago, Chile.

Seth Baum holds a Ph.D. in geography from Penn State University. He lives in New York City.

Jacob Haqq-Misra holds a Ph.D. in meteorology & astrobiology from Penn State University. He lives in Clayton, Delaware.

Sanjoy Som holds a Ph.D. in planetary sciences & astrobiology from the University of Washington. He lives in Sunnyvale, California.